For Magnolia's aunties

About This Book

The illustrations for this book were digitally drawn in Adobe Photoshop and then painted in Corel Painter using a Monoprice tablet. This book was edited by Andrea Spooner and designed by David Caplan and Nicole Brown. The production was supervised by Erika Schwartz, and the production editor was Annie McDonnell. This book was printed on 128 gsm Gold Sun matte. The text was set in McPea, a custom font made from the artist's handwriting.

If You Ever Want to Bring a Circus to the Library, DON'T!

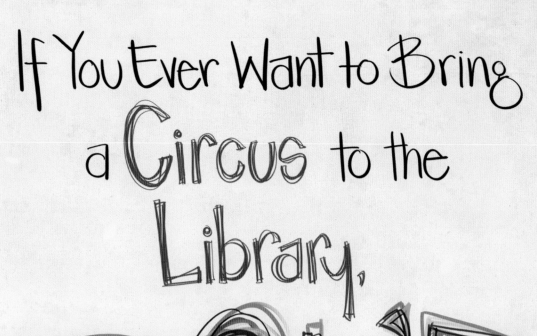

Elise Parsley

Little, Brown and Company
New York   Boston

If you see a poster that says
"YOU CAN DO **ANYTHING** AT THE LIBRARY!"
it means you can sit
and read a book
and use your imagination.

It does **not** mean
you can bring in a whole circus.

You'll tell him that it's okay
and that you know all the library rules.
This circus will be safe and fun,
and you'll only use your inside voice—
cross your heart.

You'll start by wowing the crowd as an acrobat.

You'll leap!

And twirl!

And balance
on one foot!

And twirl!

And—

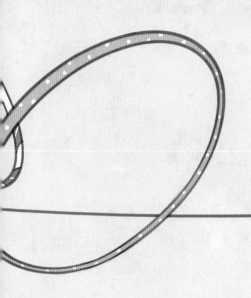

You'll tell the audience to
please hold their applause, because
YOU CAN DO **ANYTHING** AT THE LIBRARY! —
except clap.

Next up: your clown act!

You'll ask for a volunteer
from the audience
to smash a pie in your face.

You'll give your silliest look,
and she'll wind up.

That's when you'll surprise
her with your spare.

You'll have to remind the audience not to cheer.

This is a library, after all, and YOU CAN DO ANYTHING AT THE LIBRARY! — except clap and cheer.

At intermission, you'll hand out concessions. Peanuts! Popcorn! Egg-and-cheese sandwiches!

Only get this:
It turns out
YOU CAN DO ANYTHING
AT THE LIBRARY!—
except clap
and cheer
and
hand out concessions.

All right.
You didn't want to do this,
but you'll have no choice.
You have got to dazzle this
crowd, and you'll do it as
The Amazing Human Cannonball!

You'll clip on your helmet
    and warn everyone to stay back.
    Then you'll count down from ten!

Nine!   Eight!   Seven!   Six!

Five!   Four!   Three!

Two!

ONE!

Just so you know,

if your cannon is a dud,
you'll hear a kid say,
"Booo..."

You'll start to shush him, because YOU CAN DO ANYTHING AT THE LIBRARY!— except...

Booo! Booo!

Booo!

Booo! Booo!

Booo!

Booooo!

Booooo

Booo! Booo!

Booo!

By now, of course, you'll wish you were sitting and reading and using your imagination instead of leading a circus.

By now, you'd rather be **scraping gum off some chairs** than leading a circus.

You will have to think of something quick before the crowd yells for you to

Look for a way
to distract them.

You'll read about the three billy goats,
and the booing will stop.

You'll read about the
hungry old troll, and
the smiling will start.

You'll begin shouting, "WHO'S THAT TRIP-TRAPPING OVER MY BRIDGE?" and—

Sssshhhhhhhh
hhhhhhhhhhhhhh
hhhhhhhhhhhhhhhhhh
hhhhhhhhhhhhhhhhhhhhh
hhhhhhhhhhhhhhhhhhhhhhh
hhhhhhhhhhhhhhhhhhhhhhh
hhhhhhhhhhhhhhhhhhhhh
hhhhhhhhhhhhhhh
hhhhhhhhhhh
hhhhhhhh

hhhhhhhhhhhhh
hhhhhhhhhh
nh

That's when you'll know
it's time to take
your show on the road.